# FERGUS BARNABY

GOES ON
HOLIDAY

# DAVID BARROW

Fergus Barnaby lived on the
first floor with Mum and Dad.

Today was a very exciting
day because...

...Fergus Barnaby was
going **on holiday.**

Mum and Dad were busy
fussing about getting packed.

"Ready yet, Fergus?" said Dad.
"Don't forget anything!"

"I've packed my suitcase," puffed
Fergus, "and – oh, no...

My bucket and spade!
I lent them to Fred
when we were
building a fort."

Fergus Barnaby
climbed up to the
**second** floor
where Fred lived.

"Hello, Fergus Barnaby."

"Hello, Fred. I'm going on holiday. Can I have my bucket and spade?"

"Of course, here you go. Send me a photo of your best castle."

Fergus Barnaby

climbed all

the way

**down** from

the **second** floor

where Fred lived…

…to the

**first** floor

where he lived

with Mum and Dad.

He packed his bucket and spade.

"What else have you forgotten?" said Dad. He was starting to load up the car.

"Oh, no," said Fergus Barnaby. "My swimming goggles! I lent them to Emily Rose."

He climbed up to the **third** floor where Emily Rose lived.

"Hello, Fergus Barnaby."

"Hello, Emily Rose. Can I have my swimming goggles? I'm going on holiday."

"Sure thing, here you go. Practise for when we go to swimming lessons together."

Fergus Barnaby climbed
all the way
**down**
down
from the **third** floor...

...to the **first** floor where
he lived with Mum and Dad.

...past the **second** floor where Fred lived who had borrowed his bucket and spade...

He packed his
swimming goggles.

"Is there anything else you've forgotten?" said Dad checking the car.

"Oh, no," said Fergus Barnaby. "My kite! I lent it to Teddy when we were playing."

He climbed to the **fourth** floor
where Teddy lived.

"Hello, Fergus Barnaby."

"Hello, Teddy. Can I have my kite?"

"No problem, here you go. Have fun."

Fergus Barnaby climbed all the way
**down**
down
down from the
**fourth** floor…

…past the **second** floor where
Fred lived who had borrowed his
bucket and spade…

...past the **third** floor where Emily Rose lived who had borrowed his swimming goggles...

...to the **first** floor where he lived with Mum and Dad.

Fergus Barnaby packed his kite.
"Are you ready now?" said Dad.

"Oh, YES," said Fergus Barnaby.
"I think I am!"

And so they set
off on holiday.

"OH, NO!" said
Fergus Barnaby...

"**Fergus Barnaby!**" said Dad.

"You went **up** to the **fourth** floor to get **your** kite from Teddy.

You went **up** to the **third** floor to get **your** swimming goggles from Emily Rose.

You went **up** to the **second** floor to get **your** bucket and spade from Fred.

You packed your suitcase on the **first** floor where we live.

**What could you possibly have forgotten?"**

"WE'VE FORGOTTEN MUM!"

**For the real Teddy**

**With infinite thanks to Jenny & Emma
for their unwavering ingenuity**

HODDER CHILDREN'S BOOKS
First published in Great Britain in 2017 by Hodder Children's Books
This paperback edition published in 2018

A CIP catalogue record for this book is available from the British Library.

ISBN: 9781 444 92905 8

10 9 8 7 6 5 4 3 2 1

Printed and bound in China

Hodder Children's Books, an imprint of Hachette Children's Group, part of Hodder and Stoughton,
Carmelite House, 50 Victoria Embankment, London, EC4Y 0DZ

An Hachette UK Company
www.hachette.co.uk
www.hachettechildrens.co.uk